Peep Leap

by Elizabeth Verdick

illustrated by John Bendall-Brunello

AMAZON CHILDREN'S PUBLISHING

Amazon Publishing
Attn: Amazon Children's Publishing
P.O. Box 400818
Las Vegas, NV, 89140
www.amazon.com/amazonchildrenspublishing

Library of Congress Cataloging-in-Publication Data available upon request.

ISBN-13: 9781477816400(hardcover)
ISBN-10: 1477816402 (hardcover)
ISBN-13: 9781477866405 (eBook)
ISBN-10: 147786640X (eBook)

The illustrations are rendered in watercolor with colored pencils.
Book design by Katrina Damkoehler
Editor: Robin Benjamin
Printed in China
First edition
10 9 8 7 6 5 4 3 2 1

To Olivia and Zachary, my two little duckies
—E.V.

For my wonderful wife
—J.B-B.

In the hollow of a tree,
higher than the eye can see . . .

. . . nine wood ducks hatch, one by one.

"That's good!" says Mama. "We're *almost* done."

One last egg is very still. . . .

The wood ducks turn and squirm until . . .
wobble, quake, wiggle, shake—

CRAAAACK!

The smallest eggshell breaks!

"The sun is up. It's time to go."

Mama glides to the ground below,
into the pond, far and deep.
Ten baby ducks cry, *"Peep, peep, peep."*

The newborn ducks all *have* to leap,
even though the fall is steep.

Duckling ONE says, "Jumping's fun."
Mama says, "Good job! Well done!"

Then Duckling **TWO** jumps, too.
"Whew!"

Duckling **THREE** cries,
"Wait for *meeeee*. Whee!"

"And here's one more!"
calls Duckling **FOUR**.

Duckling **FIVE** does a five-star dive.

Duckling **SIX** tries some tricky kicks.

SEVEN and EIGHT call,
"We can't wait!"

NINE's next to last—but he's fast.

Into the water, one by one.
"Good!" says Mama. "We're *almost* done."

But Duckling **TEN** is quiet and still.

The wood ducks float and drift until—

Mama says, "Drop to the ground.
You can do it—safe and sound!"

Quiver, quake, shiver, shake. "Peep?"
The smallest duck is *scared* to leap.

One duck in a broken shell
isn't feeling very well.

"You are braver than you know.
Ready," says Mama. "Get set. GO!"

The deep pond shines in the sun.
Swimming looks like so much *fun*.
Is it time to leave the nest?
Can he jump and join the rest?

Maybe if he counts to three. . . .

"ONE,
TWO,
THREE!"

He's still in the tree!
"I'm stuck!" cries the baby duck.
Mama says, "Try again. Count down from ten."

...1!

LEEEEEEAP

Flap-flap

Flip-flop

Plip-plop

Safe stop.

ONE through NINE rush to his side.
All TEN ducklings dip and glide,
up and down,
'round and 'round,
in their new pond home.

AUTHOR'S NOTE

Have you ever seen a duck in a *tree*? If you're near a pond in the woods on a springtime morning, it could happen. Look up and you might spot a pair of wood ducks. They often nest high in a tree hollow near a pond, swamp, or marsh. Wood duck nests may be fifty feet off the ground—as high as a city building. The mother wood duck stays in the nest protecting the eggs, but the male, or *drake*, does not. Unlike other ducks, wood ducks don't quack. Listen for a call that sounds like a rising *jeeeeee*—that's the male. Females squeal (*oo-eek*) or sound an alarm call (*cr-r-ek, cr-e-ek*).

On hatching day, the ducklings emerge from the eggs damp and helpless. Within hours, they're dry, fluffy, and able to use their legs. In the nest, the ducklings stumble and tumble, eager to move. But they must get some rest for the big event the next day.

As the sun rises the next morning, the mother leaves the nest and lands outside. She will call to her babies only when it's safe. Then it's time for them to take a giant leap. The ducklings must jump to the ground without any help from their mother or father.

Depending on the location of the nest, the ducklings fall to a patch of earth below or right into the water. Why don't they just *fly*? Because their wings aren't fully developed—and they can't fly. One by one, the ducklings drop. *Peep?* Leap!

In the air, the ducklings are so light they flip and spin, like leaves dancing in the wind. The baby ducks have soft bones and weigh next to nothing. So when they land on the ground, they almost seem to bounce. Then off they go, following their mother to their new home in the water.

—*E.V.*